FAIRY TALE PHONICS

SAL AND THE THREE-LETTER SPELL
A TALE OF SPELLING

by Rebecca Donnelly
illustrated by Carissa Harris

Tools for Parents & Teachers

Grasshopper Books enhance imagination and introduce the earliest readers to fiction with fun storylines and illustrations. The easy-to-read text supports early reading experiences with repetitive sentence patterns and sight words.

Before Reading

- Discuss the cover illustration. What do readers see?

- Look at the picture glossary together. Discuss the words.

Read the Book

- Read the book to the child, or have him or her read independently.

- "Walk" through the book and look at the illustrations. Who is the main character? What is happening in the story?

After Reading

- Prompt the child to think more. Ask: Consonant-vowel-consonant (CVC) words are three letters long. They have consonants at the beginning and end and a vowel in the middle. Look around. What objects near you are CVC words? Spell them out.

Grasshopper Books are published by Jump!
5357 Penn Avenue South
Minneapolis, MN 55419
www.jumplibrary.com

Library of Congress Cataloging-in-Publication Data

Names: Donnelly, Rebecca, author.
Harris, Carissa, illustrator.
Title: Sal and the three-letter spell: a tale of spelling by Rebecca Donnelly; illustrated by Carissa Harris.
Description: Minneapolis, MN: Jump!, Inc., [2023]
Series: Fairy tale phonics | Includes index.
Audience: Ages 5-8
Identifiers: LCCN 2022030771 (print)
LCCN 2022030772 (ebook)
ISBN 9798885242752 (hardcover)
ISBN 9798885242769 (paperback)
ISBN 9798885242776 (ebook)
Subjects: LCSH: Readers (Primary) | LCGFT: Readers (Publications)
Classification: LCC PE1119.2 .D677 2023 (print)
LCC PE1119.2 (ebook)
DDC 428.6/2–dc23/eng/20220629
LC record available at https://lccn.loc.gov/2022030771
LC ebook record available at https://lccn.loc.gov/2022030772

Editor: Eliza Leahy
Direction and Layout: Anna Peterson
Illustrator: Carissa Harris

Printed in the United States of America at Corporate Graphics in North Mankato, Minnesota.

Table of Contents

In This Book:

You will find consonant-vowel-consonant (CVC) words. CVC words are three letters. They start and end with a consonant and have a vowel in the middle. Can you find the CVC words on each page?

Hint: A few CVC words are: **cat**, **sip**, and **log**. See if you can spot them!

Sal, Pip, and the Cup of Cocoa

Sal walks with his pigeon, Pip.

They are in the deep, dark woods.

"Let's go this way, Pip!" says Sal.

5

Sal and Pip see a cottage.

A cup of cocoa sits in the window.

Pip starts to sip it.

"No, Pip!" says Sal. "That is not yours to sip!"

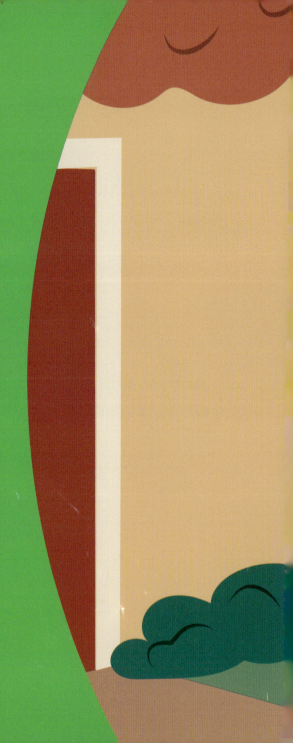

"It is mine!" says a witch. "You will pay for that."

The witch waves her wand at Pip. "Zip! Zap! Cat!" she cries.

Now Pip is a cat!

Pip waves her paw. "Meow!"

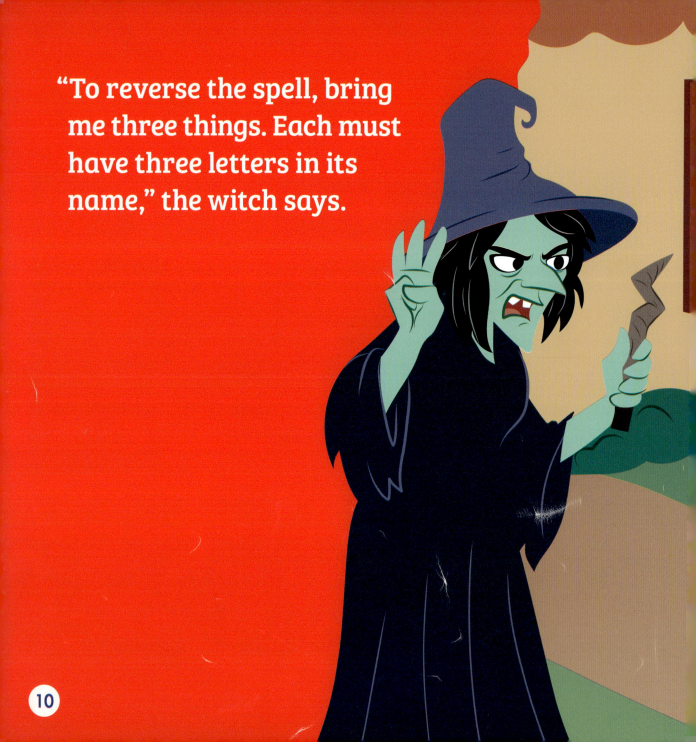

"To reverse the spell, bring me three things. Each must have three letters in its name," the witch says.

Sal looks around. He sees a tree, a leaf, and a rock.

"Those all have four letters," says Sal.

"Meow!" says Pip.

"A log!" says Sal. "You are a smart cat!"

log

Next, they find a pond.

"Pond has four letters," says Sal. "And I can't carry a pond! Fish has four letters. And a fish is too slippery."

fish

nut ▸

"Meow!" says Pip.

"A nut!" says Sal. "You are a very smart cat!"

"We need one more thing," says Sal. "What could it be?"

"Meow!" says Pip. She points to herself.

"You are the smartest cat ever!" says Sal.

cat

17

Sal and Pip bring the log and the nut to the witch.

"What is the third thing?" asks the witch.

"Meow!" says Pip.

"Cat has three letters," says Sal.

"Very well," says the witch.

Zap!

Pip is a pigeon again!

"Let's go home," says Sal.
"If we find another cup
of cocoa, let it sit!"

Let's Review!

Log and **cat** are consonant-vowel-consonant (CVC) words.
Point to the CVC words below.

leaf

sip

nut

cup

Sal

witch

paw

Picture Glossary

cottage
A small, simple house.

pigeon
A bird with a plump body, short legs, and gray and white feathers.

reverse
To make something the opposite of what it was.

slippery
Smooth or wet and very hard to hold on to.

spell
Words or a formula believed to have magical powers.

wand
A thin rod or stick used by a witch or wizard.

Index

To Learn More

Finding more information is as easy as 1, 2, 3.

❶ Go to www.factsurfer.com

❷ Enter "**Salandthethree-letterspell**" into the search box.

❸ Choose your book to see a list of websites.